THE GOLDEN WEAPONS

ADAPTED BY TRACEY WEST

ISBN 978-0-545-40115-9
LEGO, the LEGO logo, the Brick and Knob configurations and the Minifigure are trademarks of the LEGO Group.
© 2012 The LEGO Group. Produced by Scholastic Inc. under license from the LEGO Group.
Published by Scholastic Inc. SCHOLASTIC and associated logos
are trademarks and/or registered trademarks of Scholastic Inc.
12 11 10 9 8 7 6 5 4 3   12 13 14 15 16 17/0
Printed in the U.S.A.   40
First printing, March 2012

SCHOLASTIC INC.
NEW YORK   TORONTO   LONDON   AUCKLAND
SYDNEY   MEXICO CITY   NEW DELHI   HONG KONG

THE SWORD OF FIRE

"Hooray! We kicked their bony backsides!" Jay said.

Jay, Cole, Kai, and Zane were celebrating. They had defeated the skeleton warriors three times. Now they had three of the Weapons of Spinjitzu. They just needed one more.

Even Sensei Wu was in a good mood. He got up and danced.

Later, while everyone slept, a voice woke Kai. It was his sister, Nya! But how? Samukai had captured her and taken her to Garmadon in the Underworld.

"I have to go," Nya said. She ran off.

Kai raced after her. He followed her to a red temple.

Inside the temple, Kai saw the fourth Weapon of Spinjitzu: the Sword of Fire. Nya appeared in front of it.

"Nya!" Kai cried. He ran toward her.

"Don't worry, I'm right here," Nya said. But as she spoke, she transformed . . . into the dark shadow of Garmadon!

Garmadon moved aside, and Kai saw his real sister hanging above a pit of lava!

"In your world, I can't take the Sword of Fire," Garmadon said. "But you can take it for me."

Nya started to slide down toward the lava. Kai knew there was only one way to save her. He had to take the Sword and cut the chains.

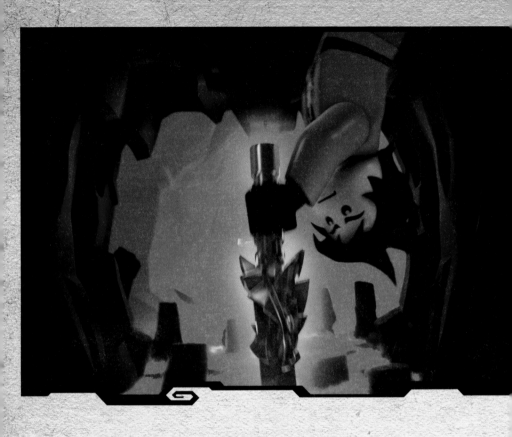

Kai grabbed the Sword.
"Ninjago!" he cried.
He swirled and whirled, turning into a glowing, red tornado. Then he flew over the lava. He cut the chains and grabbed Nya. They landed safely on the rocks.

LORD GARMADON'S PLAN

Garmadon's shadow rose up in front of Kai. He swung the Sword, but it went right through the shadow! Then Garmadon kicked Kai, and Kai fell down.

"That's not fair!" cried Nya.

Garmadon's shadow made copies of itself. All the shadows attacked Kai. The Sword fell out of his hands.

Garmadon picked up the Sword. Then a new shadow jumped behind him. It was Sensei Wu!

The sensei used his own shadow to fight Garmadon's shadows. He got the Sword back.

"But what of the other three Weapons?" Lord Garmadon asked.

"They are safe!" Sensei Wu replied.

"Are you sure?" asked Garmadon.

Back at camp, a noise woke Cole. He gasped.
Skeleton warriors Nuckal and Kruncha had
captured Jay and Zane! Their king, Samukai,
held the three Weapons of Spinjitzu in his bony
hands.

"I believe these belong to Lord Garmadon
now!" he said, grinning.

Back in the temple, Sensei Wu turned to Kai and Nya. "My brother must not unite the four Weapons," he warned them.

"Awaken, Guardian of the Sword!" Garmadon yelled. "Do not let them escape!"

A huge red dragon rose up from the bubbling lava. It spread its wings and roared.

A TRIP TO THE UNDERWORLD

There was only one escape — down into the Underworld.

Sensei Wu used the Sword to cut the rock beneath his feet. The rock floated on the lava, carrying him away.

"Sensei, no!" Kai cried.

"I must take the Sword of Fire to the Underworld," Sensei said firmly.

"I will see you there, brother," Garmadon said, and his shadow disappeared.

"It's all my fault!" Kai wailed. "Sensei won't be able to hold out for long."

"Forget Sensei," said Nya, looking up at the angry dragon. "What about us?"

Back at camp, Samukai jumped into his Skull Truck. "To the Underworld!" he cried.

The skeleton warriors sped away, leaving Cole, Jay, and Zane behind.

"Now what?" Cole asked.

"Now we get out of here," Jay answered. He drew a sword he had taken from Nuckal. He cut the rope, and they all hit the ground.

The ninja raced after Samukai. They jumped onto the Skull Truck.

Smack! Pow! Cole went after Nuckal and Kruncha. Jay ran up and . . . *whack!* Cole accidentally hit him in the throat.

The Skull Truck reared up on its back wheels. Jay, Cole, and Zane tumbled off. The truck vanished into the Underworld.

Jay, Cole, and Zane ran to the red temple.

"I sense that the Weapons are in the Underworld," Zane said. "We are too late."

Then they heard Kai's voice. "We may not be able to cross over to the Underworld," he said, "but a dragon can."

The temple doors opened. The ninja gasped when they saw Kai and Nya riding the Fire Dragon!

DRAGON RIDERS

"Dragons belong to both worlds, so they can travel between them," Nya explained.

Cole shuddered. "No way!" He was terrified of dragons.

Kai jumped down and patted the dragon's head. "Once he realized we were trying to protect the Sword of Fire, he became quite a softie!"

Nya said good-bye to her brother. Soon the
four ninja were flying across the sky, each one
riding an elemental dragon.

"Easy, easy!" Cole said nervously, as the Earth
Dragon soared across the sky.

"This is awesome!" Zane cried from the back
of the Ice Dragon.

The dragons flew through the long, dark tunnel that led to the Underworld. They saw Garmadon's black palace in the distance. Skeleton warriors guarded the entrance.

"Sensei is inside," Zane said. "And they're expecting us."

To get past the warriors, the four ninja swung from the black rocks that hung down over the Underworld. Jay grabbed onto a long and skinny rock. He looked up — and saw that it was the leg of a giant spider!

"Brak, bleck, blah!" Jay cried, but his throat was still hurt. His friends didn't understand him.

The other ninja finally looked up and saw the spiders.

"Aaaahhhh!" they screamed. They let go and fell to the ground. In an instant, the skeleton warriors had surrounded them. Then the spiders dropped down.

"Uh-oh!" Kai cried.

A BATTLE BETWEEN BROTHERS

Inside the palace, Sensei Wu heard a voice behind him.

"Brother," Garmadon said.

Sensei Wu spun around. He drew the Sword of Fire.

"Brother," he said.

"Seize the sword!" Garmadon yelled.
Skeleton warriors jumped out of the
shadows. Sensei Wu used Spinjitzu. A golden
tornado swirled around the room, knocking
down the skeletons one by one.

"You'll have to take it from me!" Sensei Wu
told his brother.

Samukai appeared. "My pleasure!" he growled, waving the other three Weapons of Spinjitzu. He let out a loud roar and charged at Sensei Wu.

The old man somersaulted right over Samukai's head. He swung the sword at Samukai, but the skeleton blocked it with the Scythe of Quakes.

TORNADO OF CREATION

Outside, the ninja needed a plan. Jay knew what to do.

"Brawr, blech, blah!" he cried.

"You need a vacation?" Kai asked.

Frustrated, Jay yelled as loud as he could. "Tornado of Creation!"

"Let's do this," said Cole. "Earth!"

"Fire!" yelled Kai.

"Ice!" cried Zane.

"Lightning!" shouted Jay.

"Ninjago!" yelled all four ninja. The four tornados burned brightly. Then they joined together. . . .

One giant, swirling tornado whipped through the palace courtyard. It picked up every warrior, spider, and object in its path. Then the tornado spat them out.

Now they were all transformed . . . into a giant Ferris wheel made of bones! The skeleton warriors were trapped inside.

"Come on! There's no time to waste!" Kai cried.

SHOWDOWN WITH LORD GARMADON

The four ninja hurried into the palace. They saw Sensei Wu battling Samukai.

Sensei Wu fought hard, but it was one Weapon against three. Samukai used the Shurikens of Ice to freeze the Sword. Then he used the Scythe of Quakes to shake the ground. Finally, he hurled the Nunchuks of Lightning at Sensei Wu, shocking him.

The Sword fell out of Sensei Wu's hands.

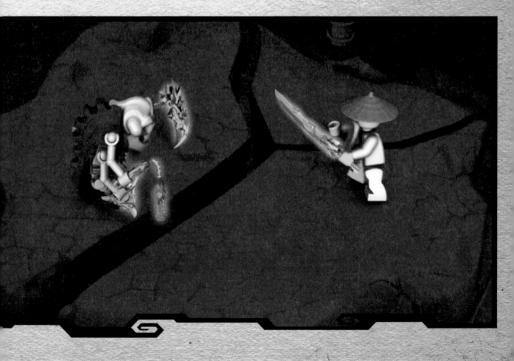

"Bring me the four Weapons," Garmadon demanded.

Samukai picked up the Sword. "No! You will obey me now!" he told Garmadon.

The Weapons began to shake and glow. Garmadon laughed.

"No one can handle all that power at once," Sensei Wu said.

"What's happening to me?" Samukai
wailed.

"You have fallen into my master plan,"
Garmadon replied. "Not even I can handle
the power of all four Weapons. But now
that they have combined, it will create a
vortex through space and time. I can finally
escape the Underworld!"

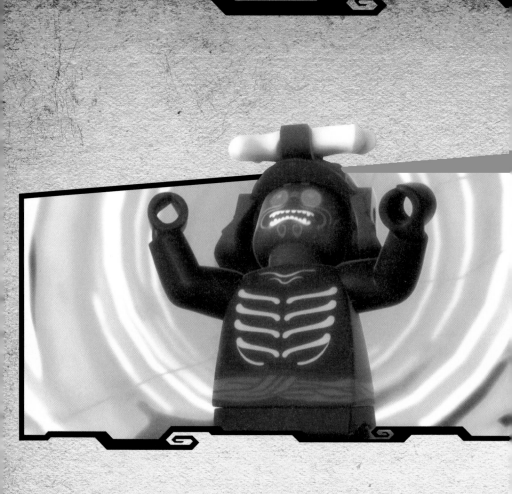

Boom! Samukai vanished in a storm of white light. A glowing blue tunnel appeared. Garmadon went toward it.

"Soon I will be strong enough to hold the four Weapons!" he boasted. "Then I will make the world in my image!"

The vortex disappeared — and so did Garmadon.

"He is gone," Sensei Wu said. "But he will return."

Kai picked up the Sword of Fire. Jay picked up the Nunchuks. Cole grabbed the Scythe, and Zane took the Shurikens. "Then we'll be ready for him!" Kai vowed.